# MANNERS

## ALIKI

GREENWILLOW BOOKS, NEW YORK

*An Imprint of HarperCollinsPublishers*

Watercolor paints, colored pencils, and a black pen were used for the full-color art. The text type is ITC
Symbol; hand lettering was done by the artist. Manners. Copyright © 1990 by Aliki Brandenberg. All rights
reserved. Manufactured in China by South China Printing Company Ltd. For information address HarperCollins
Children's Books, a division of HarperCollins Publishers, 10 East 53rd Street, New York, NY 10022.
www.harperchildrens.com
First Edition  11  12  13  SCP  20  19  18  17  16  15  14  13  12  11

Library of Congress Cataloging-in-Publication Data
Aliki. Manners/Aliki.  p.  cm.  "Greenwillow Books."
Summary: Discusses manners and gives examples of good manners and bad manners.
ISBN 0-688-09198-9 (trade). ISBN 0-688-09199-7 (lib. bdg.) ISBN 0-688-04579-0 (pbk.)
1. Etiquette for children and teenagers.  [1. Etiquette.]  I. Title.
BJ1857.C5A39 1990  395'.122—dc20  89-34622  CIP  AC

For my mother,
Stella Lagakos Liacouras

# MANNERS

# WHAT ARE MANNERS?

Manners are the way people behave.

Manners are the way you treat others.

Good manners  make you nice.

They make others  want to be with you.

With good manners, you are polite.

You are thoughtful and considerate.

Manners are WORDS and ACTIONS that show others you CARE

# WHAT BABIES DON'T KNOW

Babies are not born with manners.

They do not know how to say *Please!*

or *Thank you!* or *I'd like my Teddy!* or *I'm sleepy!*

Babies cry for things because they can't talk.

But babies grow into children, and learn.

They learn manners so others will want them around.

## NOBODY LIKES TANTRUMS!

*You know it!*

# GREETINGS

How do you do?

Good Morning,
Mrs. Lambros.

Hello!

Please
come
in.

Please
have
a seat.

Would you
like a drink?

It was a
pleasure
to meet you.
Goodbye.

It was nice
to see you
again.
Goodbye.

Goodbye.
See you
tomorrow!

# WHAT ELENA KNOWS

Please
may I
lick the
bowl?
I promise
to eat
all my
supper!

"Please"
goes a long
way.

For that,
Elena will
probably get
a cookie, too.

# MANNERS LESSON #1

*Aunt Bessie Doesn't Have to Know Everything*

# YOU ARE INTERRUPTING AGAIN, LEON

# I'M SORRY

# MANNERS LESSON #2

## The Sand Castle

# THE GRABBER

# MANNERS LESSON #3

*Too Loud Is Too Loud*

# LOOK AT DANIEL

DON'T YOU WISH YOU DIDN'T HAVE TO?

Here's a hanky, Daniel.

# HOW ANTHONY ALMOST RUINED DIANA'S PARTY

Anthony never says hello.

He has no manners.

He embarrasses.

He makes fun.

He's a bad sport.

He cheats.

He bites.

He calls people names.

He grabs.

He tattles.

He throws food.

He's rude.

He didn't even say good-bye.

Nobody missed him.

He almost ruined my party.

But he didn't.

# GOSSIP
## and
## WHISPERS

# NOBODY'S PERFECT

# OUCH

Here comes Alexa.
Let's ignore her.

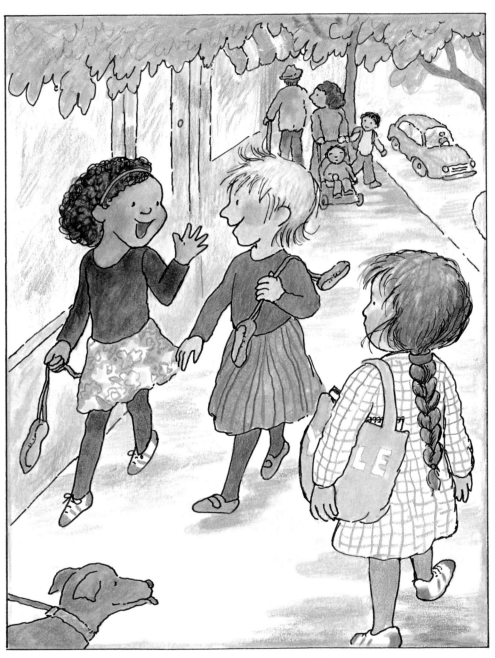

Bad manners
and
bad feelings.

Is Alexa
going to go
home and cry?

# MANNERS LESSON #4

## At the Table

Seen but not heard.

# MANNERS LESSON #5

## Part One: Wrong Number

# Part Two: Telephone Talk

# MANNERS LESSON #6

## Traveling

# PLEASE, I CAN HELP

A lack of manners
in certain places
can bother others
and cause red faces.

# PARDON AND EXCUSE ME

# MANNERS LESSON #7

## Sleep-over

# EVERYBODY MISSES YOU

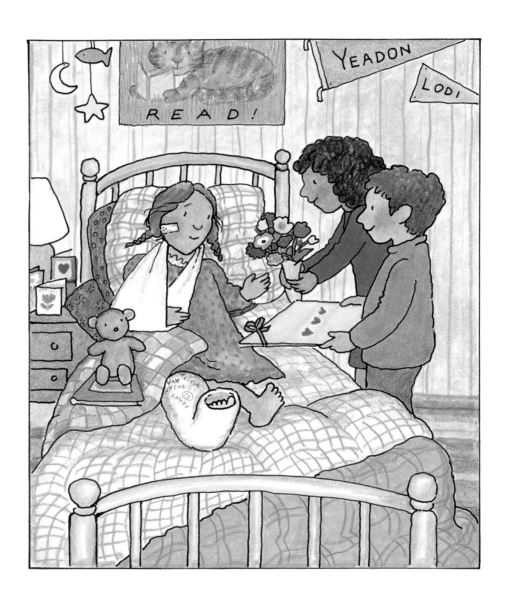

That's nice to know.

# AND NOW FOR SOME ETIQUETTE

# AFTER YOU

Wait for the hostess to begin before you do.

Offer others before you help yourself.

Wait for everyone to finish before you clear the table.

Let others enter before you.

Speak only after someone has finished.

Wait for your turn. It will come.

AFTER YOU means you think of others before you think of yourself.

# THANK YOU AGAIN

A letter is like a book.
It can be read again and again and again....